Martha
the Doctor
Fairy

To Anne-Marie, a true helper

Special thanks to
Mandy Archer

ORCHARD BOOKS

First published in Great Britain in 2015 by Orchard Books
This edition published in 2016 by The Watts Publishing Group

1 3 5 7 9 10 8 6 4 2

© 2016 Rainbow Magic Limited.
© 2016 HIT Entertainment Limited.
Illustrations © Orchard Books 2015

HiT entertainment

A CIP catalogue record for this book is available from the British Library.

ISBN 978 1 40834 887 1

Printed in Great Britain

MIX
Paper from
responsible sources
FSC® C104740

The paper and board used in this book are made from wood from responsible sources

Orchard Books
An imprint of Hachette Children's Group
Part of The Watts Publishing Group Limited
Carmelite House, 50 Victoria Embankment, London EC4Y 0DZ

An Hachette UK Company
www.hachette.co.uk
www.hachettechildrens.co.uk

Martha
the Doctor
Fairy

by Daisy Meadows

The Fairyland Palace

Seeing Pool

Tippington Hall

Tippington Town

Rachel's House

Jack Frost's
Ice Castle

Aunt Lesley's
Surgery

The Fire Station

Tippington Park

The Leisure Centre

Jack Frost's Spell

These silly helpful folk I see
Don't know they could be helping me.
But they will fail and I will smirk,
And let the goblins do the work.

I'll show this town I've got some nerve
And claim rewards that I deserve.
The prize on offer will be mine
And I will see the trophy shine!

Contents

Medical Matters

"I love springtime," said Kirsty Tate, gazing out of the kitchen window with a dreamy expression on her face. "Everything looks as if it's been washed fresh and clean."

She finished drying the plate in her hands and passed it to her best friend,

Rachel Walker, to put away. Kirsty was spending half term in Tippington with Rachel and her family.

"Thanks for helping me, girls," said Rachel's dad, Mr Walker, who was washing up after the delicious breakfast he had made. "Many hands make light work."

"It's strange that Aunt Lesley didn't join us for breakfast," said Rachel, looking at the clock. "She's usually ready to leave for the surgery by now."

"How long is she going to be staying with you?" Kirsty asked.

"Just until the building work on her house is finished," said Rachel. "I hope it takes ages – I love having her here!"

"You're so lucky," said Kirsty. "She's amazing – I wish I had an aunt who was a doctor."

Rachel stacked a couple of glasses in the cupboard and then gave a little skip on the spot, feeling excited.

"It was brilliant hearing all about her work yesterday, wasn't it?" she said.

"Yes," Kirsty agreed, smiling, "and I loved learning how to take my own pulse with the second hand of my watch. I'm so glad that she's been nominated for the Tippington Helper of the Year Award."

The Helper of the Year Award was given to someone who had done something wonderful for the Tippington community.

"She's bound to win," said Rachel. "She's such a wonderful doctor."

"Well, the other nominees are wonderful too," murmured Mr Walker with a smile. "We can't be sure that Aunt Lesley will win."

"I can," said Rachel in a determined voice. "She's unbeatable!"

Mr Walker laughed.

"You're right," he said. "I'm very proud

of her too. The most important thing of all is that her patients love her. That's the sign of a really good doctor, you know."

They finished the drying up and putting away, and then sat down at the table to practise taking their pulses again.

"Aunt Lesley's going to be late if she doesn't get up soon," said Rachel as she gazed at the kitchen clock.

"Why don't you two take her breakfast up on a tray?" said Mr Walker. "I bet she'd really be glad of that."

Kirsty went to get a tray, while Rachel filled a bowl with cereal and poured out some orange juice. They made some toast and added it to the tray with butter and honey, and then Rachel led the way upstairs and Kirsty carried the tray.

"Aunt Lesley?" called Rachel, knocking on the door of the spare room. "We've brought your breakfast up."

"Thank you, how kind!" said Aunt Lesley from inside. "Come in."

The girls opened the door. To their surprise, Aunt Lesley was still in bed. She was propped up with pillows, writing something and looking very relaxed.

"Are you working on the talk you're giving at the surgery later?" Kirsty asked, putting the tray down on Aunt Lesley's lap.

"Talk?" Aunt Lesley repeated in an

absent-minded way.

"Yes," said Rachel. "You told us all about it yesterday – how you're going to explain all the things that doctors do in the community."

"Oh, hmmm," said Aunt Lesley. "No, this is a crossword puzzle. Do you know a six-letter word meaning a person who makes people well?"

"Doctor," the girls said in unison, exchanging a worried look.

"Aunt Lesley, are you OK?" asked Rachel. "Shouldn't you be getting ready for work?"

"I don't feel like going to the surgery today," her aunt replied.

"But your patients need you," said Kirsty, feeling shocked.

Aunt Lesley just shrugged as if she

didn't care.

"Do you feel poorly?" asked Rachel.

She put her hand on her aunt's forehead, but it wasn't hot. Kirsty took her pulse, but Aunt Lesley barely seemed to notice. Kirsty shook her head and pulled Rachel to one side.

"Your aunt's not poorly," she said in a low voice. "But she's not herself either. Whatever is the matter with her?"

A Trip to the Seeing Pool

"Oh no!" exclaimed Aunt Lesley.

The girls looked around in surprise.
Had she realised that her patients needed
her?

"What's wrong?" Rachel asked.

"My pen's run out of ink," said Aunt
Lesley with a groan. "This is terrible –
how can I finish my crossword? Oh girls,

please would you run down and get
another pen from my medical bag in the
hall?"

The girls
nodded and
hurried back
downstairs,
feeling worried.

"I've never seen
Aunt Lesley like
this before,"
Rachel
whispered.
"Usually she
can't wait to go to work."

Kirsty crouched down beside the bag
and undid the catch.

"It's as if she's turned into a different
person," she said. "Yesterday she couldn't

stop talking about how much she loves being a doctor. Oh!"

Kirsty jumped up as a tiny fairy came fluttering out of the bag. Her red-gold hair was tied up with a blue ribbon, and she was wearing a white coat over her blue dress. A stethoscope was hanging around her neck.

"Good morning, Rachel and Kirsty," said the fairy. "I'm Martha the Doctor Fairy, and I need your help."

"Hello, Martha," Rachel whispered.

"We've just got to take a pen upstairs to my aunt. There's something not quite right with her this morning."

"I know all about your aunt," said Martha, nodding.

Before they could ask what she meant, the girls heard Aunt Lesley calling down from her room.

"Never mind about the pen," she said. "I'm going to go back to sleep. I feel like a nice long lie-in."

"Oh dear," said Rachel with a sigh.

"This isn't like Aunt Lesley at all."

"What did you mean when you said that you know all about Rachel's aunt?" Kirsty asked Martha.

"I can explain everything if you will come with me to Fairyland," said Martha.

The girls clasped each other's hands and nodded, smiling. No matter what the reason, it was always exciting to travel to Fairyland and visit their secret fairy friends.

While the girls pulled on their shoes and backpacks, Martha glanced around to check that no one was watching.

"It's OK," said Rachel. "Mum's gone out with a friend and Dad's making a cup of tea in the kitchen."

"Then let's go!" said Martha.

She flicked her wand and a dazzling swirl of sparkles surrounded the girls. They tingled with excitement as their wings appeared and they shrank to fairy size. Then fairy dust whooshed them into the air. One moment they were standing in the little hallway of Rachel's house, and the next they were blinking in the brilliant Fairyland sunshine.

"Welcome, girls, and thank you for coming," said a familiar voice.

It was Queen Titania, and she was smiling at Rachel and Kirsty. The girls curtsied at once.

"We're always glad when we can visit Fairyland," said Kirsty.

Looking around, they saw that they were standing beside the queen's Seeing Pool, in the grounds of the Fairyland Palace.

"Martha said that she needs our help," Rachel said.

"We all do," said a tinkling voice.

Rachel and Kirsty saw that three other fairies were standing beside the Seeing Pool.

"These are the other Helping Fairies," said Martha, stepping forward. "Girls, meet Ariana the Firefighter Fairy, Perrie the Paramedic Fairy and Lulu the Lifeguard Fairy."

The three fairies smiled at the girls.

"Queen Titania told us that you would come," said Ariana.

"Yes, you see, we don't know what to do," added Perrie. "Usually we help others, but now *we're* the ones who need help."

"What do you mean?" Kirsty asked.

"It's our job to take care of people who look after others in their community," Lulu explained. "But without our magical objects, we can't help the everyday heroes like Rachel's Aunt Lesley do their jobs. We can't help *anyone*. It's awful."

"Let me guess," said Rachel, frowning. "Jack Frost has stolen your magical objects? He's such a menace!"

The Helping Fairies nodded and Queen Titania raised her wand.

"Let's see if we can find out what he's doing now," she said.

Murmuring a powerful spell, she waved

her wand over the still water of the
Seeing Pool. It rippled and then a blurry
picture appeared.

"It's Jack Frost!" Rachel exclaimed as
the picture came into focus.

The Ice Lord was sitting at the top
of a snowdrift, and a crowd of goblins
was jostling for space below. Across his
chest was a satin sash in royal blue, with
the words 'HELPING
HERO' in large
white letters. As
the girls watched
he puffed out
his chest and
pointed to the
sash.

"Who do you
think is going to win

the Tippington Helper of the Year Award this year?" he bellowed at the goblins.

They scratched their heads, stared at each other and shrugged their shoulders.

"The Mayor?" suggested a knock-kneed goblin.

"A donkey?" said another.

"Me, you nincompoops!" Jack Frost shrieked. "ME! ME! ME!"

A Sneaky Scheme

The goblins clapped and cheered.

"But how can *you* win an award for helping people?" piped up the smallest goblin, who was rather cheeky. "You're not really going to *help* people, are you?"

"Yuck, don't be disgusting," said Jack Frost. "I'll use the Helping Fairies' magical objects to make sure I win and everyone else FAILS! And besides, I've got all of you."

The goblins beamed with pride.

"We *are* very important, it's true," the smallest goblin squawked.

"Rubbish," said Jack Frost with an unpleasant smile. "But you're going to be doing the jobs of all the people nominated for the award, so that I can take the credit. That way *I* can win the award without actually having to help anyone!"

The watching fairies gasped, but the silly goblins didn't seem to understand that this meant more work for them. They clapped and cheered, and Jack Frost sat and laughed at them.

"What do you want us to do first?" asked one of the goblins.

"Each group of goblins must come and collect one of the magical objects," Jack Frost ordered. "Then push off to the human world and win that award for me!"

The silly goblins clapped and cheered again, and then started to scramble up the slippery snowdrift. Jack Frost handed the smallest goblin a chunky white watch.

"My magical watch!" cried

Martha.

The second group, led by the knock-kneed goblin, took Ariana's magical helmet. The third group, led by another goblin, took Perrie's magical flashing siren. The remaining goblins, who were all rather pimply, took off with Lulu's magical whistle.

"He's got all our magical objects," said Perrie with a groan.

"So *that's* what's wrong with Aunt Lesley," Rachel realised. "She's stopped wanting to look after people because the magical objects have been stolen."

Martha nodded. "My magical watch makes sure that doctors give people good advice," she said. "Without it, doctors won't even *want* to help their patients."

"Now disappear to the human world and get to work!" Jack Frost squawked, waving his wand.

The goblins vanished with a blast of icy magic. Then the picture in the Seeing Pool started to shiver and break up, and Queen Titania lowered her wand.

"That's all I can see," she said in a sad voice. "I cannot tell where the goblins have been sent. All we can know for sure is that they are somewhere in Tippington."

"Then we need to get home straight away," Rachel said.

"So you'll help us?" asked Lulu.

"Of course," said Kirsty. "We'll do everything we can to get your magical objects back before the prize is awarded."

"In that case, there's no time to lose," said Martha. "Back to Tippington!"

She flourished her wand and the girls were once more surrounded by swirls of fairy dust. A few moments later, feeling a little dizzy, Rachel and Kirsty were standing in a narrow alleyway.

"We're human-sized again," said Kirsty.

"Yes, and we're back in Tippington," Rachel replied.

37

"This is the alleyway next to Aunt Lesley's surgery. Why have you brought us here, Martha?"

Martha was fluttering beside them, biting her lip and looking anxious.

"I think this is where the goblin with my magical watch will come," she said. "Jack Frost sent the goblins to do the jobs of all the people nominated for the award."

"We have to try to keep the goblins away from Aunt Lesley's surgery," said Rachel. "They could cause all sorts of mischief!"

Martha hid inside Kirsty's backpack, and then the girls walked out of the alleyway and up the steps to the surgery. As soon as they pushed the door open, they were stopped in their tracks by the noise. The waiting room was filled with patients who were grumbling, shouting, coughing and sneezing. Each one was holding a number, and the receptionist was trying to keep them all calm, enter their details into the computer and answer the phone – all at the same time.

"Hi, Uma," said Rachel, walking up to the reception desk.

"Oh Rachel, I'm so glad to see you," said Uma. "Is your aunt feeling better? Her talk is due to start soon, and the replacement doctor is giving patients some… er… very strange advice!"

Crazy Cures

Just then, a man came out of the examining room, hopping on one foot. Uma stood up and looked at him in surprise.

"Excuse me, sir," she called after him. "I don't remember you hopping when you went into the room – I thought you came in for a cold. Are you all right?"

"I soon will be," said the man. " The doctor says it'll cure my cold in an hour."

"See what I mean?" said Uma as the man left the surgery and the next patient went into the examining

room. "I've never heard a doctor say that before."

Kirsty and Rachel exchanged glances. Was it possible that the goblins were already here? Uma asked the caller to ring back and put the phone down.

"Er, Uma, what's the new doctor like?" Rachel asked.

The phone rang again. Uma picked it up and put her hand over the receiver.

"He seems quite young for a doctor," she said. "And he has extremely large feet. Oh, excuse me, I really must answer this call."

"Kirsty, are you thinking what I'm thinking?" asked Rachel.

Kirsty nodded. "It sounds like a goblin in disguise," she said. "But we  have to get into the examining room and meet him to be sure."

Rachel looked around at all the angry patients.

"It'll take hours to get in if we join the queue," she said. "We have to do something quickly. Martha, I think it's time for us to become fairies again!"

Rachel and Kirsty slipped behind a large pot plant, and then Martha fluttered out of Kirsty's backpack and flew above the girls, waving her wand.

Dazzling fairy dust showered down on the girls, and they instantly shrank to fairy size. A few seconds later they were fluttering beside Martha and peering out from behind the pot plant.

"Look – the examining room door is opening," Kirsty whispered.

A lady walked out, singing *Hickory Dickory Dock* backwards. In the waiting room, a lady stood up and beckoned to her son.

"Come on, Josh!" she said. "It's our turn at last."

As Josh and his mum walked into the examining room, the three fairies flew in above them. The door shut, and the fairies perched on a tall cupboard.

For a moment, Rachel and Kirsty didn't even look at the doctor. They were too busy staring at the terrible mess. Papers and files were scattered all around the room. Medical equipment covered the floor and the desk, and Aunt Lesley's computer was flashing with a big warning signal.

"This is terrible," said Rachel. "Aunt Lesley always keeps her examining room neat and tidy. She'd be really upset to see this."

The girls couldn't see the doctor's face

because he was wearing a wide-brimmed hat, but Kirsty pointed to his enormous feet and nudged Rachel and Kirsty.

"His coat is much too big," she said. "I think he's a goblin in disguise."

Then they heard a
squawk from the
far corner of
the room,
and saw a
group of
other goblins
in hats and
white coats,
messing
around with
thermometers
and stethoscopes. Martha let out a
little groan.

"Ahem," said the doctor goblin, putting
on a silly, deep voice. "Sit down and, er,
start moaning… no… I mean, tell me
what's wrong."

"Isn't it obvious?" asked Josh's mum.

She and Josh sat down, and the fairies saw that he was covered in spots. The doctor goblin rubbed his hands together.

"Is it because he's so ugly?" he asked. "I can't do anything about the nose, but we could pluck his eyebrows…"

"His spots!" exclaimed Josh's mum.

"Oh yes, of course," said the doctor goblin with a nervous giggle. "Well, it's probably a cold, but I need to take his pulse."

He pulled a chunky
white watch out of his
pocket and Martha
gasped.

"My watch!" she
said, leaning forward
over the cupboard.
"It's here!"

"And we have to
get it back," Kirsty
added. "But how?"

The goblin doctor held the watch
upside down and pressed it against Josh's
forehead, before putting it carefully back
into the pocket of his coat. Josh's mum
frowned.

"I thought it was probably chickenpox,"
she said.

"That's right," said the goblin doctor.

"Chickenpox, definitely."

He nodded so much that his hat fell off. He snatched it up and plonked it back on his head. Josh's mother stared at him.

"Yes," he squawked. "Chickenpox."

"So what should I do to help him?" Josh's mother asked.

"He should stand on his head three times a day after meals," said the goblin doctor. "NEXT!"

Josh immediately leaned over as if to try straight away. But his mother pulled him to his feet.

"I've never heard such utter nonsense," she said. "I'm not coming back here again until Dr Lesley returns."

She stomped out and the goblin doctor blew a loud raspberry at her back. Kirsty tapped Martha on the arm.

"I've got an idea," she whispered. "But you'll have to turn us both back into humans again."

Rainbow Pox

A few seconds later, Rachel and Kirsty stepped out from behind the cupboard and walked up to the doctor as if they were his next patients. Rachel pretended to sneeze... and sneeze... and sneeze.

"Help!" Kirsty exclaimed. "I think my friend has sneezitis. She's sneezing nonstop – can you help her? Can you take her pulse?"

"No need for that," said the goblin doctor, waving his arm. "The best cure for sneezitis is to clap your hands and stamp your feet."

Kirsty bit her lip. The goblin doctor stared at Rachel, who kept sneezing. There was nothing else for it – she started to clap her hands and stamp her feet.

As the goblin doctor stared at Rachel, Kirsty had another idea. She whispered to Martha, who was hiding in her backpack, and the little fairy waved her wand. A ribbon of fairy dust twirled its way across the room and up the nostrils of the goblin doctor.

"AH-CHOO!" he burst out.
"AH-CHOO! AH-CHOO!"

Rachel stopped sneezing and stared
at the goblin doctor, whose eyes were
beginning to water.

"AH-CHOO! AH-CHOOO!"

"Oh my goodness, you must have
caught the sneezitis!" Kirsty
exclaimed. "Now *you're*
going to have to clap
your hands and
stamp your feet!"

As the doctor
goblin started to
clap and stamp,
Martha slipped
out of Kirsty's
backpack.

With all the sneezing, clapping and stamping, the doctor goblin couldn't see anything, and the other goblins were busy drawing pictures on prescription forms. It should have been easy for her to dive into the doctor's coat to get the magical watch. But when Martha got close to the pocket...

"AH-CHOO!" A gigantic sneeze shook the goblin doctor's body, and he moved out of Martha's way. She fluttered closer to the pocket again, but just as she was about to fly inside...

58

"AH-CHOO!" He turned to hold on to his desk. The plan wasn't working.

"We have to think of something!" cried Kirsty.

Suddenly Rachel remembered the doctor goblin's strange cure for Josh's chickenpox.

"I've got an idea!" she exclaimed. "Martha, hide under my hair and I'll whisper to you."

Martha darted out of sight, and smiled as she listened to Rachel's plan. Then she waved her wand and the goblin doctor stopped sneezing. Martha took a deep breath and chanted a quick spell.

Goblin, goblin, grow some spots.
Big ones, small ones, lots and lots.
Goblin, though your skin is green,
In rainbow colours now be seen.

With that, a rash of
rainbow-coloured spots
appeared all over the
doctor goblin's face.
Rachel gasped and
Kirsty put her hand
to her mouth.
"Oh my goodness,
you must have rainbow
pox!" she exclaimed. "It's the worst case
I've ever seen!"

Rachel pulled the goblin doctor over to
a mirror on the wall, and he gawped at
his face in horror.

"Look at me!" he shrieked at the other goblins. "Help!"

But the other goblins just pointed at him and rolled around the floor laughing. Kirsty gave him a comforting pat on the back.

"There, there," she said. "The cure for rainbow pox is the same as for chickenpox – you just have to stand on your head."

Panting and gibbering to himself about spots, the goblin doctor did a headstand. Just as Rachel had planned, Martha's magical watch came tumbling out of his pocket!

Helping Hands

"Look out!" squawked the other goblins, diving towards the magical watch.

"Too late," said Rachel, pouncing on the watch. "It's time that this was returned to its rightful owner."

As the goblins jumped up and down in fury, Martha flew out of hiding and took the watch, which magically shrank to fairy size.

The goblins groaned, but the goblin doctor was on his feet again and gazing into the mirror.

"It hasn't worked!" he wailed. "I'm still all poxy!"

"Spots are going to be the least of your worries when Jack Frost finds out what's happened!" one of the other goblins yelled. "The fairy's got her watch back, you imbecile! Come on, we've got to hide."

The other goblins opened the window
and clambered out, but the doctor
goblin stared at Martha. His bottom lip
trembled.

"I want my
handsome
green face
back," he
whimpered.

With a
wave of
Martha's
wand, the
rainbow spots
vanished. The goblin
doctor heaved a sigh of relief, and then
pulled off his white coat and hat.

"I suppose I'm not a very good doctor
after all," he said in a croaky voice.

"Never mind," said Martha with a bright smile. "I have just the thing to make you feel better."

She tapped her wand on his chest, and a sticker appeared there.

I was very brave at the doctor's today.

The goblin grinned and then followed the others out of the window. Martha turned to the girls with a little laugh.

"What an exciting morning!" she said. "Thank you from the bottom of my heart. I have a little something for you too."

She tapped their chests with her wand,
and two more stickers appeared with
rainbow-coloured writing.

Doctor's Helper

"Thank you," said Rachel, gazing at
her sticker. "It was a pleasure to help!"

"I must take my magical watch back
to Fairyland," said Martha. "But please
keep an eye out for the other three
magical objects."

"We will," Kirsty promised her.
"Goodbye!"

There was a bright, silvery flash that
made the girls shut their eyes. When
they opened them again, Martha had
disappeared and the examining room was
as neat as it had always been. No one
could have guessed that goblins had been
there a few minutes earlier.

"Perfect," said Rachel. "Come on, let's go home and wake Aunt Lesley up."

They went back into the waiting room, but they were surprised to see that all the patients had disappeared. Instead, the waiting room chairs were laid out in rows, and people were filing in to take their seats for the talk. Uma smiled at the girls and beckoned them over to the reception desk.

"I've just been speaking to your aunt," she said. "Wonderful news! She's feeling much better and she's on her way to work!"

68

An hour later, Kirsty and Rachel were sitting in the front row as Aunt Lesley came to the end of her talk. Every seat was filled, and some people were even crowding around the edges of the waiting room so they could listen.

"Finally, I would like to say that one of the most important things you need to be a good doctor is to love what you do," said Aunt Lesley. "Nothing gives me more happiness than helping my patients to feel better."

Everyone burst into applause and Aunt Lesley made her way over to the girls.

"Will you help me?" she asked them. "I want to show the children in the audience how to take a pulse and use a stethoscope."

"Of course," said Rachel and Kirsty at once, feeling proud to be asked.

As they started to demonstrate to the other children, they saw Josh's mother tap Aunt Lesley on the shoulder.

"That was a wonderful talk," she said. "I was wondering – what do you think about standing on your head as a cure for chickenpox?"

The girls flashed a smile at each other, and Aunt Lesley laughed.

"I can't say I've ever heard of it," she said. "Chickenpox usually gets better on its own, but I can give you some special lotion for the itching."

"Thank you, that would really help," said Josh's mother. "Good luck for the Tippington Helper of the Year Award."

As Josh's mother walked away, Rachel had an idea. She looked up at her aunt.

"Aunt Lesley, we'd really like to meet the other nominees for the award," she said. "Do you think that might be possible?"

"Of course," said Aunt Lesley at once. "They're all lovely people. I'll take you this week."

She turned aside to speak to Uma, and Kirsty squeezed Rachel's hand.

"Good thinking," she said. "It's brilliant that Martha has got her magical object back, but we've still got three more objects to find."

Rachel nodded. "We have to make sure that helpers in the community are there for the people who need them," she said. "Hopefully we'll be able to find the other magical objects very soon!"

Meet the
Storybook Fairies

Can Rachel and Kirsty help get their new fairy friends'
magical objects back from Jack Frost, before all
their favourite stories are ruined?

www.rainbowmagicbooks.co.uk

Now it's time for Kirsty and
Rachel to help...

Ariana the Firefighter Fairy

Read on for a sneak peek...

The kitchen was filled with the clatter
of cups and plates and the smell of toast
– the Walker family had just finished
breakfast.

"It's another gorgeous spring day,"
said Rachel Walker, stepping out of her
back door into the garden. "I'm so glad
we don't have to sit inside a classroom
today."

Her best friend, Kirsty Tate, followed her
and took a deep breath of fresh air. She
was staying with Rachel in Tippington
for half term. The kitchen window
opened and Mrs Walker leaned out to

call to them.

"Girls, please would you water the plants while you're out there?" she asked. "They need extra care in all this heat."

It had been a wonderfully sunny half term so far. Rachel and Kirsty filled their watering cans and started to water the beautiful plants. The spring bulbs were flowering and scenting the air.

Just as Kirsty was watering the tulips, she heard a faint sound. Rachel heard it too, and stopped beside the daffodils to listen.

"It's a meow," said Kirsty. "There must be a cat in the garden. Come on, let's find it!"

They put down their watering cans and searched among the bushy plants and behind the plant pots, but there was no sign of a cat. Then Bailey, the little boy who lived next door, popped his head over the fence. He looked worried.

"Rachel, please will you help me?" he called. "My kitten, Pushkin, has climbed on top of the shed in your garden, and now she's stuck!"

"Of course we will," said Rachel at once. "Don't worry, Bailey – we'll get her down."

Read Ariana the Firefighter Fairy to find out what adventures are in store for Kirsty and Rachel!

Calling all parents, carers and teachers!
The Rainbow Magic fairies are here to help
your child enter the magical world of reading.
Whatever reading stage they are at, there's
a Rainbow Magic book for everyone!
Here is Lydia the Reading Fairy's guide to
supporting your child's journey at all levels.

Starting Out

1 Our Rainbow Magic Beginner Readers are perfect for first-time readers who are just beginning to develop reading skills and confidence. Approved by teachers, they contain a full range of educational levelling, as well as lively full-colour illustrations.

Developing Readers

2 Rainbow Magic Early Readers contain longer stories and wider vocabulary for building stamina and growing confidence. These are adaptations of our most popular Rainbow Magic stories, specially developed for younger readers in conjunction with an Early Years reading consultant, with full-colour illustrations.

Going Solo

3 The Rainbow Magic chapter books – a mixture of series and one-off specials – contain accessible writing to encourage your child to venture into reading independently. These highly collectible and much-loved magical stories inspire a love of reading to last a lifetime.

www.rainbowmagicbooks.co.uk

"Rainbow Magic got my daughter reading chapter books. Great sparkly covers, cute fairies and traditional stories full of magic that she found impossible to put down" – Mother of Edie (6 years)

"Florence LOVES the Rainbow Magic books. She really enjoys reading now" Mother of Florence (6 years)

The Rainbow Magic Reading Challenge

Well done, fairy friend – you have completed the book!
This book was worth 5 points.

See how far you have climbed on the **Reading Rainbow** on the Rainbow Magic website below.

The more books you read, the more points you will get, and the closer you will be to becoming a Fairy Princess!

How to get your Reading Rainbow
1. Cut out the coin below
2. Go to the Rainbow Magic website
3. Download and print out your poster
4. Add your coin and climb up the Reading Rainbow!

There's all this and lots more at
www.rainbowmagicbooks.co.uk

You'll find activities, competitions, stories, a special newsletter and complete profiles of all the Rainbow Magic fairies. Find a fairy with your name!